Jodie the Juggler

Written by Vivian French

Illustrated by Beccy Blake

Collins

Jodie loved juggling.

He juggled with his socks.

He juggled with his shoes.

He juggled with three oranges and ...

... he broke a cup.

"Jodie," Mum said, "go outside and play football."
Jodie didn't want to play football.
He wanted to juggle.

He went outside and juggled with three flower pots and ...

... the flower pots broke!

Mum yelled, "JODIE, STOP JUGGLING!"

Jodie went up to Asif's flat.

Jodie showed Asif how to juggle.

They juggled with Asif's socks.

They juggled with Asif's shoes.

They juggled with three apples and ...

CRASH!

... they broke a plate.

"Boys," said Asif's dad, "go outside and play football."
Jodie didn't want to play football. He wanted to juggle.

Jodie went back down to his own flat.

Mum was in the kitchen making a cake.

"No juggling!" said Mum, as Jodie picked up three eggs.

But it was too late.

The eggs broke!

"Jodie," sighed Mum, "we're going to the park to play football NOW!"
Mum carried the football. Jodie wanted to juggle.

Dom, Sue and Ash were in the park.

They ran over to Jodie.

"Can we borrow your football?" they asked.

"Yes," said Jodie. "I don't like football.

But I'll try one kick first."

He took the ball from Mum and
kicked it as hard as he could.

up and up

Up went the ball,

and up.

Down came the ball,

down and down

and down ...

DANGER
KEEP OUT!

... it smashed some glass!

"BRILLIANT kick!" gasped Dom.

"A golden goal!" yelled Ash.

"You're a STAR!" cried Sue.

"Jodie," said Mum firmly, "we're going home."

Mum and Jodie walked home slowly.

"Sorry, Mum," Jodie said quietly.

"Lucky that man gave us our ball back."

Mum said, "Maybe juggling *is* a good idea.

I'll make you some juggling bags."

Jodie looked at her and smiled a huge smile.

"I don't want to juggle any more," he said.

"I want to play football!"

A table

Game	
 juggling	a cup
football	some glass

What Jodie broke

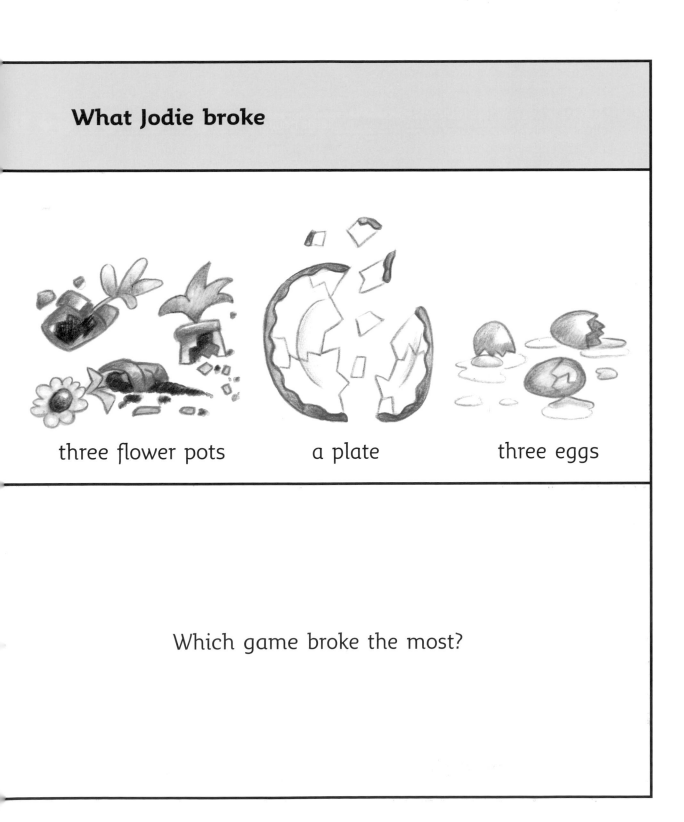

three flower pots   a plate   three eggs

Which game broke the most?

⦂ Ideas for guided reading ⦂

Learning objectives: to read longer phrases and more complex sentences; attend to a range of punctuation; listen to others, ask relevant questions and follow instructions; understand time and sequential relationships in stories; use awareness of grammar to decipher new words.

Curriculum links: Physical Education: Games and activities

High frequency words: he, with, his, and, a, mum, said, go, play, didn't, to, went, three, come, on, in, how, they, dad, back, down, own, was, as, up, but, it, too, going, now, were, over, don't, one, took, ball, from, could, some, you, I, like

Interest words: Jodie, juggling, flower pot, kitchen, sighed, carried, wanted, borrow, brilliant, gasped, yelled, cried

Word count: 330

Getting started

This story may be read over two sessions.

- Look at the front cover and read the title. Ask who can juggle (Jodie). Ask the children to read the blurb on the back cover together. Use the picture on the back cover to encourage children to predict what Mum's big surprise might be.

- Read pp2–4 together. Model how to use the picture (a flying orange!), and the grammar of the broken sentence (*'He juggled with three oranges and ... he broke a cup.'*) to help predict the next event.

- Walk through the rest of the story up to p21, looking at the pictures and discussing what is happening. How does Jodie's mum try to stop Jodie juggling?

- Point out the use of speech bubbles as part of the story on pp6–7.

Reading and responding

- Ask the children to read the story quietly and independently. Observe each child read aloud and praise for fluency and attention to punctuation. Praise their use of grammar to decipher new or unfamiliar words, e.g. to predict from the text; to read on; to leave a gap and re-read.

- Encourage the children to use the sense of the sentence to aid expression, and to read the speech bubbles as part of the story.

- Check the children are using a range of strategies to tackle challenging words: looking at the pictures; sounding out words; looking for familiar patterns and endings.